P9-DNA-335

Simon Fairfield Public Library
PO Box 607
Douglas, MA
01516

WITHDRAWN

Cinderella Smith

The Super Secret Mystery

by

Stephanie Barden

Illustrations by

Diane Goode

HARPER

An Imprint of HarperCollinsPublishers

Also by Stephanie Barden
Cinderella Smith
Cinderella Smith: The More the Merrier

Cinderella Smith: The Super Secret Mystery
Text copyright © 2013 by Stephanie Barden
Illustrations copyright © 2013 by Diane Goode
All rights reserved. Printed in the United States of America.
No part of this book may be used or reproduced in any manner
whatsoever without written permission except in the case of brief
quotations embodied in critical articles and reviews. For information
address HarperCollins Children's Books, a division of HarperCollins
Publishers, 10 East 53rd Street, New York, NY 10022.
www.harpercollinschildrens.com

Library of Congress Cataloging-in-Publication Data is available.
ISBN 978-0-06-200443-7

Typography by Erin Fitzsimmons
13 14 15 16 17   LP/RRDH   10 9 8 7 6 5 4 3 2 1
❖
First Edition

To
all the schools, students, teachers, and librarians who have
welcomed me and Cinderella Smith into your classrooms.
Especially Sunny Hills Class of 2013,
Seattle Country Day, Villa Academy, Bertschi,
View Ridge, and Wedgwood.
And to my own elementary school,
Laurelhurst, for inspiration
—S.B.

For Peter
—D.G.

1

Ladybug Boots

"**D**o you ever think about what you want to be when you grow up?" I asked my best friend, Erin.

"All the time," she said. "Right now I think I might want to be a scientist like my stepdad. What do you want to be?"

"I'm not sure," I said. "But I definitely don't want to be a school bus driver."

"Why not?"

"Because being on school buses makes me a little sick to my stomach."

"Let's change seats," said Erin. "Sometimes being

by the window helps. Also, look out, not in."

I rubbed the fog off the window with my hand and looked outside. The sky was all full of dribbly-spit, which is not good field trip weather. *Alas.*

"Do you feel better?" Erin asked after a few minutes.

"What's wrong?" Charlie had poked his head over from the seat behind us.

"Cinderella feels a little sick," said Erin.

"Is she going to throw up?" he asked.

"No," I said.

"Maybe we should open the window, just in case." Charlie reached over and tried to push it up.

"What's going on?" asked Jack, Charlie's seatmate.

"Nothing," I said.

"Cinderella's feeling sick," said Charlie.

"We need a barf bag at the back of the bus!" yelled Jack. "Cinderella's going to blow!"

"I am not," I said.

"Cinderella, that's disgusting." Rosemary T. leaned across the aisle. And FYI, Rosemary T. and I used to be friends, but we're not so much anymore.

"Don't get too close!" Rosemary W., Rosemary T.'s best friend, pulled her back into her seat.

"Is everything okay back there?" our teacher, Mr.

Harrison, called from up front.

"Everything's fine," I called back.

"Cinderella's about to throw up!" Rosemary T. yelled at the same time.

"I am not!" I said.

"She is not!" said Erin.

"It looks like she is," said Rosemary W.

"I'm *fine*," I said to the Rosemarys.

"Are you sure?" Mr. Harrison walked to the back of the bus, even though you're not supposed to get out of your seat when the bus is moving. He looked at me very concerned.

"I'm positive," I said. "I felt a little sick for a minute, but now I'm just fine and dandy." With everyone making such a big deal of it, I was for sure going to be fine and dandy too.

"Okay, but let me know if you start to feel bad again." Mr. Harrison walked back up to the front. "We'll be at the zoo in about five minutes."

"I can't wait to get there," I said to Erin. "And not because I was feeling sick. Just because it's one of the best places ever."

"I know," said Erin. "I love the zoo, especially the penguins."

"Me too," I said. "And the meerkats and the red

pandas and the Komodo dragons."

"And everything in the Day House." Zachary leaned over the back of his seat in front of us.

"You shouldn't get too close to Cinderella," said Rosemary T. "She's probably highly contagious."

I did a big, huge sigh, and Erin and I rolled our eyes at each other.

"I'm not scared of her," said Zachary.

I gave him a thumbs-up, and he gave me one back and bumped my knuckles with his.

"Hey," I said, "that's vexylent! A thumbs-up-bump!"

"Don't you dare start making up words again," said Rosemary T.

I like to make up words and try to get them in the dictionary. A couple weeks ago I made up *vexylent*, which means "very, extremely excellent." I guess she thought *thumbs-up-bump* was a new one I was trying out.

"Thumbs-up-bump! Thumbs-up-bump!" Erin and Zachary and I chanted and bumped each other at the same time.

"Now you're really getting germy, Zachary," said Rosemary T. "Be sure to use some hand sanitizer."

"I am not," said Zachary.

"Neither am I." Charlie stuck his head right between me and Erin and patted me on the head.

"Cut it out, Charlie," I said.

Then the bus stopped and the door hissed open and a zoo person jumped on. She did a *clap, clap, clap-clap-clap*, and we did one back and then got quiet.

"Wow." She sounded pretty impressed. I guess not everyone knows about clapping back and then listening. "Welcome to Woodland Park Zoo. Are you Mr. Harrison's third-grade class?"

"Yes!" we all said.

"Here to learn about endangered animals?"

"Yes," only a few of us said. I guess some kids forgot why we were here.

"Okay," said the zoo person. "Follow me, and we'll go see some animals!"

"Yay!" everyone yelled, and we filed off the bus.

"Are you the last one?" the zoo person asked.

5

"Yep," I said. "Sorry if you had to wait. I took my boots off on the ride over, and it took me a little while to get them back on."

She looked down at my feet. "Those are great boots."

I looked down at my rain boots too. "Thank you. I picked bright red with black polka dots so they would be harder to lose."

"You could put your name on them too. That's what I do with my hats." She took her hat off and showed me the inside, where it said "Robin Chrispin."

"I always put my name and address on the bottoms." I grabbed on to Erin and kicked my leg out in front to show her.

"Cinderella?" Robin read the name off the bottom of my boot.

"It's just my nickname," I said.

"Because she loses shoes a lot," said Erin.

"But they get returned to me this way," I said.

"Glad to hear it," said Robin. "Follow me, everyone." We walked along a curvy path, and I knew we were heading to the Tropical Rain Forest area. I was very, extremely familiar with the zoo because my whole family likes it here. Robin stopped in front of a big glass window.

"I don't see anything," said Rosemary T.

"It's the gorilla exhibit," I said.

"I know *that*," she said. "But where are they?"

"They're probably hiding from you," said Jack.

"Harrumph!" said Rosemary T.

Just then the gorillas came out. We watched them wander around their exhibit, picking up lettuce and other vegetables that were scattered all over.

"Can anyone tell me why gorillas are endangered?" asked Robin.

"Mainly because of limited resources," said Logan.

"What's that mean?" asked Zachary.

"It means they're running out of the things they need to survive," said Logan. "Like places to live and food to eat."

"I'm impressed," said Robin. "You know your stuff."

"I'm doing my endangered species report on gorillas, and I already have some notes," said Logan.

I was impressed too. I hadn't thought much about the report yet, but maybe I should start.

"Let's move on."

7

We followed Robin to the next exhibit.

"The animal that lives here is pretty shy, so keep your voices low," said Robin.

"I just saw some leaves move!" yelled Zachary.

Everyone shushed him.

A big, beautiful jaguar pushed through some bushes. It stood on the other side of the glass looking right at me. Everyone crowded around and *ooh*ed and *aah*ed very quietly.

"Move, Cinderella," hissed Rosemary T. "I want to see better."

I stepped back and crashed into Rosemary W.

"Ooh!" Rosemary W. yelled, and the jaguar moved away from the glass.

"Good job, Rosemary W.," said Charlie.

"Let's be quiet, and he'll come back," said Robin. "Why do you think jaguars are endangered?"

"Because of their beautiful fur." Rosemary W. pushed right up next to Rosemary T.

"Yes," said Robin. "Any other reasons?"

"Also their limited resources," said Rosemary T.

"Exactly," said Robin. "They're hunted for their fur and are losing their habitat. Many other animals are too, like gorillas, as we discussed before."

We went into the Tropical Rain Forest building.

It was warm and wet, and people's glasses got all fogged up.

"Now that we're inside we can spread out and explore at our own pace," said Robin.

"Grab a buddy and take notes in preparation for your reports," said Mr. Harrison.

Erin grabbed me and I grabbed her, and we headed off.

"What lives here?" Erin asked the Rosemarys, who were standing in front of a big glass window.

"Nothing," said Rosemary T.

"We've been here for hours," said Rosemary W. "It's empty."

"We've only been in the building for a few minutes." I sat down in front of the exhibit.

"You probably weren't patient enough." Erin walked over to the sign, and the Rosemarys huffed away.

"It says a highly endangered ocelot lives here." Erin kept reading, and I took a ton of notes.

"I think I see it!" From where I was sitting, I could

see a tail hanging down from a tall branch.

"It was really blending in up there." Erin sat down next to me, and we started sketching.

"Hey, maybe that's what happened to my missing leopard-print flat," I said. "Maybe it's camouflaged somewhere."

"We'll go on a search next time I'm over," said Erin.

"And we won't look inside this time," I said. "We'll look all over the garden and places outside."

The next exhibit was full of hissing cockroaches, which were not endangered so we didn't spend much time with them.

"We're taking a poll." Christopher and Trevor were standing in front of a snake exhibit. "Would you rather trip over a boa constrictor or a bushmaster?"

"Neither." Erin walked over to the next cage, where two toucans were sitting on a branch.

"Hmm." I thought for a minute. "I'd rather trip on a boa constrictor. At least I'd have a chance of staying alive with that guy."

"Excellent answer," said Christopher. "The bushmaster's venom would be the end of you, but you might be able to elude the constrictor."

"Phew!" I hurried to catch up to Erin.

We tried to sketch golden lion tamarin monkeys,

but they were jumping around their cage too fast.

"They're cute," said Erin.

"But frustrating," I said.

The poison dart frogs next door were much easier to draw.

"I wish I could have one of these for a pet," said Charlie.

"But you could never play with it," I said.

"It says they lose their poison in captivity," he said.

"*Achoo!*" Jack sneezed all over the glass.

"That's disgusting!" said Erin.

"Five more minutes, class," Mr. Harrison called.

We hurried to see the rest of the exhibits and took as many notes as we could.

When Robin walked us back to the bus, she had us move like the different animals we'd seen. We hopped like frogs and slithered like snakes and swung through the trees like monkeys, even Mr. Harrison. The only ones who didn't were the Rosemarys and Hannah.

"You look so weird and dumb," said Rosemary W.

"And immature," said Rosemary T.

I almost told them that what's really weird and dumb and immature is not doing something fun because of how it looks. Instead, though, I just ignored them. It took me a while to figure it out, but sometimes that's the best thing to do.

Lots About Ocelots

"I think today was the best school day of the whole year," I announced during dinner.

"Better than the spelling bee day?" asked my dad.

"Definitely," I said. "There is nothing better in the whole wide world than a field trip to the zoo."

"What was your favorite animal this time?" he asked.

My favorite animal always changes, so that's why he asked the question that way.

"I think probably the jaguar," I said. "He walked right up to the glass where I was standing and looked at me. I'm not going to do my report on him, though."

"Why not?" My mom brought us each a bowl full of sliced pears. *Alas.* Pears are just fine and dandy, but I always hope for something not so healthy for dessert.

"It's all due to limited resources," I said.

"What's that?" My little sister, Tess, turned her plastic brontosaurus around so it could share her pears.

"It means there's not enough of something for everyone to get what they need," I said. "We learned all about it at the zoo today. Right now I'm talking about library books, though, not food and water and things like that. I bet lots of people are doing their reports on jaguars, and that means all the books on them will get checked out."

"Couldn't you use other sources of information?" asked my dad.

"The rules for the report are: two sites from the internet, two books from the library, and one encyclopedia article."

"Why do the books have to be from the library?" asked my mom.

"I think Mr. Harrison and Ms. Pearl, the librarian,

are in a little bit of cahoots."

"What's 'cahoots'?" asked Tess.

"It means they're secretly working together," I said. "I think they want to make sure all the third graders know how to check out books before Thanksgiving."

"Ah," said my mom. "So what animal are you going to do?"

"An ocelot," I said. "It was lying way up high on a tree branch, but it kind of looked like a jaguar. Except it was the size of Miss Purvis." And Miss Purvis, by the way, is my aunt Flora's cat, who I just love.

"Does it make a noise like Miss Purvis?" asked my dad. Miss Purvis is a very loud, yowly cat.

"I'm not sure," I said. "I didn't hear it make any kind of noise. I've got a lot of research to do."

"When is the report due?" asked my mom.

"The week before Thanksgiving." All of a sudden that didn't seem very far away. "May I be excused? I think I'll get started."

"Certainly," said my mom.

I slid out of my chair and headed to the computer.

"Don't forget to clear your plate," called my mom.

I came back and piled my bowl and glass and fork

and napkin all onto my plate. I think it is just a waste of time to make more than one trip to the dishwasher. As soon as my stuff was loaded in, I got the notebook that I'd brought to the zoo and sat down at the computer. While I waited for it to warm up, I wrote *Lots About Ocelots* in big, puffy letters on the cover.

"Can I help?" Tess came into the living room.

I didn't really want her help, but we have a rule in our house. Whenever you can say yes, say yes. It just makes life easier.

"Yes," I said, and I didn't even sigh.

She pulled a chair up next to me and set her brontosaurus on the desk, facing the screen.

I typed in *ocelot* and started clicking onto different sites. "I'm going to print up a whole bunch of ocelot pictures to glue onto the front of this notebook."

"I wish I had homework." Tess is turning four soon and just can't wait to start preschool.

"Can you go get me scissors and a glue stick?" I asked.

"Sure!" Tess jumped off her chair and ran out of the room. After a few minutes, she walked back in slowly, holding her fist around the blade end of the scissors, just like I'd taught her. I gave her a thumbs-up, and she gave me one back with her other hand.

"Let me show you something cool." I bumped her thumbs-up knuckles with mine. "It's called a thumbs-up-bump."

"Awesome," she said.

"While these pictures are printing, I think I'll draw an ocelot on the inside. I tried to draw one at the zoo, but I didn't have a very good view."

"You need colors." Tess slid off her chair and raced out of the room. "Here!" She set a big box of crayons on the desk next to her brontosaurus.

I kept sketching, and she pulled out crayons and held them up to the ocelot on the screen. "You need whitey-yellow and orange and black."

The colors she picked out were perfect. I gave her a thumbs-up and she gave me one back, and we thumbs-up-bumped a few times. Then I got back to work, printing and sketching and gluing and filling my notebook with lots about ocelots.

3

Puppy Tooth-Marked Clog

"**A**fter we finish lunch, let's go to the library instead of outside to play." Erin handed me another French fry, and I handed her another mini rice cake. "These are good. What flavor are they."

"White Cheddar," I said. "Did you pick your animal yet?"

"I'm still not sure between toucans or golden lion tamarins," said Erin. "As soon as I decide, though, I'm going to make a notebook like yours."

I'd brought my *Lots About Ocelots* notebook to lunch to show Erin, and it was sitting on the table between us.

"What's that?" Hannah and Abby walked by our table on the way to where the Rosemarys were sitting.

"It's a notebook I'm working on for our report," I said.

Abby stopped and looked closer at the cover, but Hannah race-walked over to the Rosemarys.

I opened it up and showed Abby my sketches and notes.

"I'm going to make one too," said Erin.

"That's vexylent," said Abby. "When I pick my animal, can I make one?"

"Certainly!" I smiled big, because one, she liked my notebook idea. And two, my word, *vexylent*, was definitely catching on.

After we finished eating, we headed up to the library. Some kids from our class were already

there, and Ms. Pearl assigned us to computers right next to Zachary.

"Are you working on your report too?" I asked.

"Yep," said Zachary. "I'm trying to find an animal. My favorite is a hamster, but they're not endangered."

"Maybe you could find a tropical rain forest hamster-ish animal," I said.

"Good idea." Zachary started searching on his computer.

Erin typed in *toucans* on hers. Three books popped up, and she wrote down their titles. Then she typed in *golden lion tamarins*. This time six different book titles appeared.

"Look at this," said Zachary. "It's the world's biggest rodent called a capybara."

Erin and I looked over at his computer screen.

"Awesome," said Erin. "You should do that."

"I can't," said Zachary. "It's not endangered."

"Well, that's sort of one of those good-news, bad-news things then," I said.

On my computer, I typed in *ocelot*. Five books came up, and I started to write down all the titles, but then I thought about limited resources. "All our books are in the same section. Let's just go and look, because some might be checked out already."

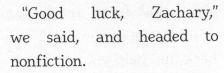

"Good luck, Zachary," we said, and headed to nonfiction.

There were four whole shelves of animal books. Erin started pulling out bird books looking for toucans, and I started pulling out cat books looking for ocelots. Pretty soon Erin had three: one just about toucans, one about birds in the rain forest, and one about birds of the world.

"Hey, look at this guy!" Zachary called over to us.

We race-walked over to where he was sitting. We didn't want to call back to him because we were in the library, after all.

"He's called a Pacific pocket mouse." Zachary pointed to the computer screen.

"He's so cute," we both said at the same time.

"I'm definitely going to do him," said Zachary. "What are you doing, Erin?"

"Toucans," said Erin. "I'm not even going to look at golden lion tamarins, because I already found three good book resources."

"I haven't found anything yet," I said.

"I'll go check these out," said Erin, "then I'll come back and help you."

The books about cats were all on the bottom shelf. I kneeled down on the floor and slipped off my puppy tooth-marked clogs so I could concentrate better. There were tons about lions and tigers and cheetahs and pet cats. I looked and looked, but I couldn't find anything on ocelots. I decided I needed an expert. I went over to the library desk, where Erin had just finished checking out her books.

"Ms. Pearl," I said. "I think I need some help. I can't seem to find anything on ocelots."

Ms. Pearl led the way back to the nonfiction section. "If these are your shoes, you were in the right place."

My cheeks got a little warm, and I quick slipped back on my clogs.

Ms. Pearl ran her fingers along the spines of the books. "You're right; there's nothing here. Let's go see what we can figure out."

We followed her back to her desk, and she typed into her computer. "It looks like books on jungle cats are very popular at the moment. One of your classmates checked out three of them, and another checked out the other two."

"Hmm," I said.

"Do you want to pick a different animal?" asked Ms. Pearl.

"It's a little too late," I said. "I already started on my report."

"I see," she said. "The books are due back Monday. Can you wait until then?"

I thought for a minute. "I guess so. I can do my online resources and my encyclopedia article. Maybe I can even draw more pictures until they get turned back in."

The end-of-recess bell rang, so we headed to class with Zachary.

"I wonder who checked out the books," I said.

"Yeah," said Zachary. "Who else is doing ocelots?"

"Erin!" Ms. Pearl stuck her head out the library doorway. "Can you come back for a minute? I forgot to slip these in your books." She held up three bright yellow DUE BACK IN THREE DAYS cards.

"Sure," Erin called back to her. "If I'm late, can you tell Mr. Harrison I'll be right there?"

"Yessiree," I said, and kept walking with Zachary.

When we were just about to our room, we met up with the line of the rest of our class and Mr. Harrison.

"*Oooooh,*" said Jack. "Cinderella and Zachary sitting in a tree . . ."

"We were in the library," I said, very disgusted.

"*K-i-s-s-i-n-g,*" said Jack.

"We were checking out books," I said even more disgusted.

"First comes love, then comes . . ." Charlie and Jack said together.

"That's enough, Jack, Charlie," said Mr. Harrison.

I gave Charlie mean stink eyes. Jack always did stuff like that, but Charlie didn't.

"Okay, everyone," said Mr. Harrison. "We have about twenty minutes before we go to PE. Read silently at your desks or work on your reports."

Trevor and Christopher stood a whole bunch of books around the edge of their desks like a wall.

"What in the world are you up to?" I asked.

"Excellent question," said Mr. Harrison. "What in

the world *are* you up to?"

"We don't want anyone to know what animal we're doing for our reports," said Christopher. "We want it to be a surprise."

"Yeah," said Trevor. "We want to shock and amaze you! We want to shock and amaze the whole class!"

"I see," said Mr. Harrison.

And then the rest of the class must have decided they wanted to shock and amaze everyone too. Walls of books started going up everywhere.

I looked over at Logan, who sat right next to me, but he wasn't standing any books up.

He shrugged his shoulders. "Everyone already knows I'm doing gorillas, because I told at the zoo."

I shrugged my shoulders right back. "A couple people know what I'm doing, but it's still mostly secret." I pulled *Mrs. Frisby and the Rats of Nimh* out of my desk. "I don't have any books on my animal yet, though, so I'm just going to read for fun."

"I have tons of books on gorillas," said Logan, "but I think I'll just read for fun too." He opened up one of my all-time favorite books, *A Wrinkle in Time.*

"That is a vexylent book." I gave him a thumbs-up.

He looked at the cover of mine. "So is that one."

He gave me a thumbs-up back, and I bumped his knuckles.

"That's called a thumbs-up-bump," I said.

Just then Charlie walked by with a pencil in his hand. "I know what animal you're doing your report on."

"You do?" I asked.

"Yeah." Charlie pointed to the cover of my book. "You're doing rats." He sort of danced and sang over to the pencil sharpener. "Cinderella's doing rats! Cinderella's doing rats!"

"No she's not," said Rosemary T. "She's doing ocelots! Hannah told me!"

"Now you can't shock and amaze anyone!" said Jack.

I started to get frustrated and mad and sad all together, and that's an awful lot to keep inside at

the same time.

"Are you going to start crying?" asked Jack.

"No." I blink, blink, blinked very hard.

"Maybe the whole secret-report idea isn't such a great idea after all," said Mr. Harrison.

"Yes it is!" said Christopher.

"We have our hearts set on it!" said Trevor.

And I guess a lot of the rest of the class did too, because a whole bunch of them agreed.

Mr. Harrison looked back and forth at me and Christopher and Trevor like he didn't know quite what to do.

And all of a sudden I had an *AHA!*, which means a very, extremely good idea. Actually, I only had part of an *AHA!*, but that didn't stop me. I stood up like I was making an important announcement. "It is just fine and dandy with me if everyone keeps their animals secret. My animal isn't what's going to shock and amaze you about my report. Something else is, and you won't believe it!"

"Same for me!" Logan stood up too. "Everyone knows I'm doing gorillas, but you will be amazed by what I tell you about them!"

"Me too!" Zachary stood up at the back of the room. "I am doing the Pacific pocket mouse, and you will be very shocked by stuff!"

Mr. Harrison looked a little bit shocked and amazed by everything already. I thought he was going to ask me and Logan and Zachary to take our seats, but instead he just said, "Everyone else up too. It's time for PE."

4

Scuffed-up Pink Ballet Slippers

"**H**ow are you going to shock and amaze everyone with your report?" asked Erin.

We were leaning up against the fence, waiting to be picked up after school for dance class. A lot of other kids were around, so I whispered back, "I don't have the foggiest idea. I was just so mad and frustrated all at once that it popped out of my mouth."

"You'll be able to come up with something good," said Erin.

"I hope so," I said.

"You will," she said again. "I'll help."

Her mom pulled up in her periwinkle VW bug.

"See you in a few minutes," said Erin, and she and Emma and Nicole from the other third-grade class climbed into the car.

I looked down the fence to where Rosemary T. and Rosemary W. were

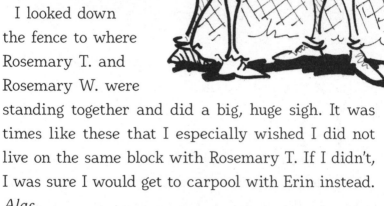

standing together and did a big, huge sigh. It was times like these that I especially wished I did not live on the same block with Rosemary T. If I didn't, I was sure I would get to carpool with Erin instead. *Alas.*

Rosemary T.'s mom pulled up, and I walked over and climbed in. Rosemary T. and Rosemary W. gave each other hugs. They acted like they weren't going to see each other ever again instead of in just a few minutes. Finally she got into the car.

"How was school today, girls?" asked Mrs. Taylor.

"It was good," said Rosemary T. "We decided to keep our endangered animals a secret. That way everyone will be shocked and amazed when we give our reports."

"That's a fun idea," said Mrs. Taylor. "What a clever teacher you have."

"It was our idea, not his," said Rosemary T. "Mr. Harrison almost wouldn't let us do it because Cinderella cried."

"I did not," I said.

"You almost did," said Rosemary T.

"I did not," I said. "I think it's a fine and dandy idea, and I'm all for it. I bet my report will be the most shocking and amazing one of all, even though you know what my animal is."

"It will not," said Rosemary T. "Mine will."

Luckily we pulled up in front of dance class right then so we didn't have to keep arguing in front of her mom.

Miss Akiyama was waiting out front, and Rosemary T. ran right by without stopping to say hi or anything. I bet she was on her way to find Rosemary W., who was coming in another carpool with Hannah and Abby.

"Hi, Miss Akiyama," I said.

"Hello, Cinderella," said Miss Akiyama. "I have one more group to wait for and then we'll get started."

I went inside to change from my school clothes to my leotard and tights.

"Do you have *both* your ballet slippers this time?" Rosemary T. stuffed her school clothes into a cubby.

"Yes." I quick looked in my ballet bag to make sure both of my scuffed-up pink ballet slippers really were inside. They were. *Phew!*

Class started with our regular warm-up at the barre. Then we moved across the floor practicing our leaps and slides. Next Miss Akiyama started teaching us the two dances we'll be doing in our Winter Wonderland Recital next month.

The first was called the dreidel dance. It was Super Fun with a capital *S* and a capital *F*! We got to wear our tap shoes and pretend to be tops and twirl all over the place.

The second one was called Falling Snow. We started by standing very still like trees. Then our branches, which were really our arms, started moving. Next the Snow Princess came, blowing all around us. The Snow Princess is a solo part, and Miss Akiyama hasn't decided who gets to be her yet.

When dance class was over, my mom and Tess were waiting out front in our car.

"Where's Rosemary?" asked my mom.

"She's saying good-bye to Rosemary W.," I said. "For some reason it takes them a long time nowadays."

Tess pushed her dinosaur over to me, and I gave it some pats.

Rosemary T. finally got in the car. "Hello, Mrs. Smith. Hello, Tess."

"Hello, Rosemary," said my mom. "How are you?"

"I'm fine," said Rosemary T. "What toy did you bring this time, Tess?"

"Brontosaurus," said Tess a little bit mean. She did not like Rosemary T., but she knew she would get in trouble if she didn't answer her.

"What's his name?" asked Rosemary T.

"Charlotte," Tess said a little growly. "She bites."

It got very quiet in the car for a few minutes until finally my mom said, "How was dance class?"

"It was very good," I said. "Miss Akiyama started teaching us our dances for the next recital. We're doing two, a tap dancing one and a ballet one."

"My favorite is the ballet," said Rosemary T. "I like the solo part."

"I think my favorite is the dreidel one," I said.

"Because you know you won't get a solo again?" I guess since I got the solo part at the Autumn Recital, Rosemary T. didn't think I'd get this one.

"No," I said. "Because tap dancing is my favorite."

"As soon as you know when the recital is, let me know," said my mom. "I'm sure your Grandmother Smith and Grandma B. and Aunt Flora will all want to be invited."

"I've already invited my mom and dad and Andrea and Libby." Andrea and Libby are Rosemary T.'s big sisters, FYI.

"I'm coming," said Tess. "So is Charlotte Brontosaurus."

"I'm also inviting my grandparents," said Rosemary T., "and all my aunts and uncles and cousins."

"You'll have quite a crowd then." My mom pulled up in

front of Rosemary T.'s house. "Could you ask your mom to let me know the date?"

"She probably doesn't remember." Rosemary T. climbed out of the car. "She's very busy with the PTA and all her charity work."

I watched my mom's eyebrow start to go up in the rearview mirror. Her eyebrow thing was usually reserved for my family and sometimes things on the TV. This time, though, I  was pretty sure she was doing it to Rosemary T., and I was pretty happy about that. Maybe she was finally figuring out Rosemary T. a little bit.

"Thank you very much for the ride, Mrs. Smith," said Rosemary T.

When my mom pulled away, I said, "Peace at last!" I figured since my mom's eyebrow had gone up, maybe I was allowed to be a little mean.

"Peace at long last," said Tess.

"That's enough, girls," said my mom. So maybe it still wasn't okay after all. *Alas.*

5

The Group in Cahoots

Erin and I headed to the library as soon as we finished lunch on Monday. While she turned in her books, I went over to the animal section to get mine. There weren't any, though.

I walked over to Ms. Pearl's desk. "For some strange reason there still aren't any books with ocelots in them."

"Let me take a look." She put her glasses on her nose and typed on her computer. "It looks like they were returned and then checked right out again."

"By the same people?" I could not believe my ears. I looked over at Erin, and she looked back at me. I could tell that she could not believe her ears either.

"No. And yes." Ms. Pearl bent closer to her computer. "The two people who checked out the books you want returned them at the same time. Then they checked out the other person's."

"When did all this happen?" I tried to raise my eyebrow up.

"I had a substitute this morning, so it must have happened then."

"So the books are gone for three more days?"

"I'm sorry, but yes," said Ms. Pearl.

"Hmm." I bit down on my fingernails and thought about all this. "We only need two books for our reports. Now these guys are both going to have five." I was starting to get a little bit nervous about finishing my report.

"Would you like me to reserve them for you?" asked Ms. Pearl. "When they come back in on Thursday, I could set them aside with your name on them."

"That would be awesome," I said. "And it would still give me plenty of time to finish my report."

"I'll leave myself a note." Ms Pearl pulled a pencil from behind her ear and wrote down my name and the books I wanted.

"Hi!" Zachary came into the library just when we were leaving.

"Hi-bye," Erin and I said at the same time.

"I wonder who has the books I need," I said. "I hope they are just really interested in jungle cats. I hope they're not in cahoots with each other."

"It's impossible to know," said Erin. "Everybody is being so secretive."

"I was going to ask Ms. Pearl who had them," I said, "but I thought maybe it was very private information, like if you get lice or something."

"That's private information?" asked Erin.

"Yep," I said. "If someone at the school finds them on your head, they just send you home and don't tell anyone at all. Last year kids kept disappearing in the middle of the day, and it was a little bit spooky. Finally we found out what was going on, though."

Erin scratched her head. "Every time I hear the word *lice* I start itching."

We sat down on our favorite bench by the basketball courts. Her itching made me start itching too. "I've never had lice, have you?"

"I did when I was in kindergarten," said Erin. "My mom said it was awful, but I don't remember it."

"Guess what?" Zachary ran over to us and jumped on the bench. "There is not one single thing on Pacific pocket mice in our whole library! It is that rare!"

"Wow!" I said.

"That's amazing!" said Erin.

"What is?" Charlie bounced his basketball over to us and started dribbling in a circle around our bench.

"None of your business!" I was still a little mad that he'd tried to tell everyone what my animal was.

"I bet it's shocking and amazing animal report stuff." The end-of-recess bell rang, and Charlie ran off to get in line.

"It is pretty shocking and amazing that there's nothing in our library," I said. "You should say that as part of your report."

"Yeah," said Zachary. "That would be good."

We slid off the bench and started walking to our line.

"What are you going to do about your resources?" asked Erin.

"I don't know," said Zachary. "Ms. Pearl said I should ask Mr. Harrison."

"Maybe you can go to a different library," I said. "Actually, maybe I can too. The books I need keep getting checked out. I'll ask Mr. Harrison and let you know."

"Take your seats, everyone," said Mr. Harrison when we got into class. "You may read silently at your desks until music or work on your reports."

I raised my hand.

"Do you have a question, Cinderella?"

"Yes, but it's a secret-y one. Can I come up there and ask?"

"Of course," said Mr. Harrison.

I walked up to his desk and said very quietly, "Zachary and I are having trouble getting the books we need for our reports at the school library. Can the book resources come from another library?"

"Sure," he said, "but why so hush-hush?"

"Everybody knows what our animals are," I explained. "We need to have some secrets."

I turned back to my desk and gave Zachary a thumbs-up.

"What did you ask Mr. Harrison?" asked Logan when I sat down.

Since his animal wasn't a supersecret either, I started to tell him; but Christopher and Trevor were listening, so I raised my hand again.

"Another supersecret question?" asked Mr. Harrison.

"No," I said. "I was just wondering if maybe me and Logan and Zachary could all sit together to work on our reports. Everyone knows our animals, but we have some other stuff to discuss that we are in cahoots about."

Mr. Harrison rubbed his hands together. "I cannot wait to see these reports. You may use the worktable at the back of the room."

Logan gathered up his books, and I grabbed my *Lots About Ocelots* notebook.

Erin raised her hand. "May I sit at the worktable too?"

"Only people who don't have secret animals can,"

said Rosemary T.

"I'm doing toucans," Erin said very loud so everyone could hear.

The class made *ooh* and *ahh* noises.

"It's no big deal," said Erin. "It's not like I have lice or anything."

Now the class made an *eew* noise.

"If it's okay with the Group in Cahoots in the back," said Mr. Harrison, "it's fine with me."

"Thumbs-up from the Group in Cahoots," I said.

Logan and Zachary and I all gave a thumbs-up, and Erin brought her toucan books back to the worktable. Once she set them down she did a thumbs-up too, and the four of us all bumped our knuckles together.

"Hey," said Zachary. "That can be our group's secret handshake."

"It's not very secret," Rosemary T. called from her table.

"Yeah," said Rosemary W. "We all saw it."

"Oh well," I said. "We have plenty of other secret things."

I leaned way into the table and so did Erin and Logan and Zachary.

"So, what did you ask Mr. Harrison?" whispered Logan.

"I asked him if we could check out books for our reports at the regular library," I whispered. "Zachary can't find anything at all at ours, and the books I need keep getting checked out."

"Why did you ask it supersecret?" asked Logan.

"I didn't want to give anyone else the idea," I said. "Because I really need to get some books."

"Maybe I'll go to the regular library too," said Logan. "I have seventy-two facts on gorillas, but I could always use more."

"Seventy-two is pretty amazing," said Zachary.

"Yeah," said Logan, "but none of them are very interesting."

"Tell us some," I said.

Logan opened up his notebook. "Fact one: there are three subspecies of gorillas. Fact two: one is the western lowland gorilla. Fact three: one is the eastern lowland gorilla. Fact four: one is the mountain gorilla."

"You're right," said Zachary. "Those aren't very interesting."

"How do you shock and amaze people with facts?" asked Logan.

"Maybe you could do them in different voices," I said.

"Are you good at accents?" asked Zachary.

"I can do a French one," said Logan. "*Bonjour, mesdams est mosures.* Fact five ees dere are only feefty-five tousand goreellas left in zee vild."

We all four laughed very loud.

"Mr. Harrison," said Rosemary T. "I can't concentrate with all the noise they're making at the worktable."

"Luckily it's time to go to music," said Mr. Harrison. "Let's line up."

6

Tie-dyed TOMS

When I ran out of school, teeny-tiny snowflakes were falling, and all the kids were running around yelling and looking happy. All the grown-ups were standing in the middle of the playground looking cold and grumpy, including my mom and Mrs. Thomas. The Thomases, by the way, live down the block from us. Louie is in kindergarten and Maggie is best friends with Tess, and we walk to school with them most every day.

"Would you mind getting Louie for me?" asked Mrs. Thomas. "I need to go corral Maggie."

"Sure!" I ran over to the kindergarten yard. It's a play area with awesome climbing stuff and a fence all around to keep little kids safe. It's not like us bigger kids are mean or anything; it's just that we play pretty hard at recess. Sometimes we run over or knock into a little kid on accident.

"It's time to head home!" I called to Louie.

"Okay!" He jumped off a pretend little bridge where I used to play the Three Billy Goats Gruff.

"I miss playing in there." I did a big, huge sigh.

"I can't wait until I'm old enough to play out there with you," said Louie. "Do you think we'll have a snow day tomorrow?"

"No," I said. "It's melting when it hits the ground. It's not sticking at all."

"Rats," said Louie. "I've never had a snow day."

"I've only had two in all the years I've been going to school," I said. *"Alas."*

"Alas," he said.

Our moms were busy talking about their book group, so I waited until we said good-bye to the Thomases to talk to my mom. She just hates being interrupted, and I wanted her to say yes to everything I was going to ask.

"Can I invite some people over after school tomorrow?"

"Sure," said my mom

"What people?" asked Tess.

"The Group in Cahoots," I said. "Otherwise known as Erin, Zachary, and Logan."

"Is that a club?" asked Tess.

"No," I said. "It's all the kids that are doing not-secret animal reports. We have to find another way to be shocking and amazing."

"Shocking and amazing?" asked my mom.

"The class decided to not tell anyone what animals they were doing their report on," I said. "They wanted to shock and amaze each other. Everyone already knew what Logan's animal was, though, and everyone found out what mine was. Then Erin and Zachary decided to tell so they could be part of our group too."

"Speaking of groups," said my mom, "I need to ask

Chris a question about the book group." Chris, by the way, is Charlie's mom.

"And speaking of books," I said, "I have another question. I'm having a little trouble getting the books I need for my report from the school library. Can you or Dad maybe take me to the regular library if I can't get them?"

"Sure," she said again.

We got to our house and I stopped, but my mom and Tess kept walking.

"Can I just be home by myself?" I asked. "Charlie called me Tinder at school today, and I do not feel like seeing him at all."

My mom thought about that for a little bit. "I suppose." She unlocked our front door. "We won't be long."

"Take as long as you need." I walked into our house and did a great, big, happy sigh. "Home at last."

I dumped my backpack by the door and kicked off my shoes. One of my tie-dyed TOMS rolled under the chest where we put mail and car keys, but I left it for later. I went out to the kitchen and made a very boring snack of raisins and saltines. Like I mentioned before, it's always healthy, healthy, healthy food around our house. *Alas.*

When I finished my raisins, I blew into the box to make that whistle sound that I just love. Someday I plan to be able to whistle all on my own. I especially plan to be able to make that really loud one that gets everyone's attention. My dad can do it, and he's teaching me. I also plan to be able to make one of my eyebrows go up like my mom does and also to have pierced ears. And when I thought of that last thing, I had a great big *AHA!*

The main reason that my mom says I can't get my ears pierced yet is because I'm not responsible enough. But here I was home all by myself, and nothing bad was happening. That was pretty responsible. I had made my own snack, and that was pretty responsible too. I could clean up my own snack and even wipe the crumbs off the table. I could also put my backpack in my room without being asked. And my shoes too. I mean shoe. There was only one. That wasn't very responsible.

Then I remembered that the other one had rolled under the chest. I reached under to get it, but that's not what I found.

"What in the world?" I pulled out two pennies, my Grandmother Smith's glasses case, a cat toy that must belong to Miss Purvis, and finally my tie-dyed TOMS. I put the pennies and glasses case and cat toy on top of the chest, then carried my backpack and shoes to my room. While I was there I picked up all my clothes off the floor and put them in my hamper. Then I started picking up all my shoes. And that's what I was doing when my mom and Tess came home. I was being a very responsible, grown-up, ready-to-get-my-ears-pierced-any-day-now girl.

7

Spyers

"I didn't know you lived this close to school," said Logan.

"Yep," I said. "It's very handy."

"She lives right next door to Charlie," said Zachary.

"And down the block from Rosemary T.," said Erin.

"*Alas,*" I said very quietly so my mom couldn't hear.

My mom and Louie turned up the Thomases' front walk.

"Is that your house?" Logan sounded impressed, and I knew why. The Thomases have a huge house with an enormous yard.

"No," I said. "It's Louie's. My little sister is playing

with his little sister. We have to drop him off and pick her up."

"Wow," said Mrs. Thomas when she opened her door. "You've got quite a crowd today."

"This is Erin and Zachary and Logan," I said. "They're coming over so we can work on our endangered animal reports."

"Are you doing a report all together?" she asked.

"No, we're each doing our own." But then I thought a little bit about that. "If we did, though, that might be kind of cool."

"It might be amazing," said Erin.

"It might be shocking too," said Zachary.

"We could each turn in our own report," said Logan, "but we could present all together."

"Yeah!" We all said at once.

We grabbed Tess and said good-bye and walked down the Thomases' front steps. Before we could even head down the sidewalk, Rosemary T. came running out of her house and crossed the street.

"What are you guys doing?" she asked.

"We are having a Group in Cahoots meeting at my house," I said.

"Can I come?" she asked.

I was so surprised by this that my mouth popped

wide-open and no words came out. Rosemary T. hadn't wanted anything to do with me at all this year. Plus, she knew she couldn't come over and listen to all the secret cahoots stuff. My mom was standing right there, though, and she was very into being polite. She always thought everyone should be included in everything. I did not know what to do, so I just stood there all quiet.

Luckily Erin talked for me. "No, you can't."

"At least not today," I said.

"Why not?" Rosemary T. asked.

"You know why," said Logan.

"Yeah," said Zachary. "You already know our animals; you can't know anything more."

"Whatever." Rosemary T. huffed back across the street and into her house.

I looked up at my mom a little worried. Both her eyebrows were normal, though, so maybe I wouldn't get a stern talking-to after everyone went home.

We sat around our dining-room table, and my mom brought in a snack of apples and Cheddar cheese rice cakes.

"Can Charlotte and me be in the cahoots group too?" Tess set her brontosaurus on the table.

"I'm a big dinosaur fan," said Logan.

Tess gave him a thumbs-up and he gave her one back, and they did a thumbs-up-bump.

"Hey," said Zachary. "She knows the secret handshake! She has to be a member!"

We all five thumbs-up-bumped each other, then I called the meeting to order.

"How far is everyone on their reports?" I asked.

"I got some facts about the Pacific pocket mouse from the internet," said Zachary. "They were supposed to be extinct, but then someone found some."

"Are they called pocket mice because they're so

small?" asked Erin.

"Or because they like pockets?" I asked.

"They have little pockets in their cheeks for storing food," said Zachary, "but I bet they like regular pockets too. My hamster loves to crawl into mine."

"You should bring it to class," said Logan. "And pretend it's a mouse."

"It's not allowed to leave my bedroom," said Zachary.

"I have a lot of toucan facts," said Erin, "but nothing very shocking or anything."

"I have eighty-six gorilla facts now," said Logan.

"I wonder how we could mash all our facts together." I stared at Charlotte Brontosaurus in the middle of the table and thought and thought. All of a sudden I had an *AHA!* "Hey, what if we brought in pretend animals and did something with them? I have a stuffed animal that sort of looks like an ocelot."

"I have a stuffed gorilla!" said Logan.

"I have Tiptoe, a Beanie Baby mouse," said Tess.

"Could I borrow it?" asked Zachary.

"Yes!" Tess climbed off her chair and ran to find Tiptoe.

"I don't have a toucan," said Erin, "but I could get one."

I grabbed up Charlotte Brontosaurus and marched her around the table. "Maybe we could do a puppet show or something with our animals."

Tess came running back into the room holding Tiptoe. *"Ahh!"* she yelled. "Spyers!" She pointed to the window.

We all turned around to look and heard a crashing noise outside. We raced to the front door and pulled it open superquick. Running down the street one way was Rosemary T. and running next door was Charlie.

"What in the world?" I yelled.

Charlie's front door slammed.

"Do you think Charlie and Rosemary T. are in cahoots?" I could barely believe what my eyes had just seen.

"It certainly looks like it," said Logan.

"And here's the proof." Zachary waded through the bushes underneath our front window and grabbed up a basketball. Charlie's basketball.

"They were spying on us!" said Erin.

"This is very, extremely shocking," I said.

"They already know our animals," said Logan. "They must have been trying to figure out what amazing thing we were going to do."

I started to see red, which means I got very, extremely mad. "You know what this means."

"War," said Zachary.

"We need to devise a counterattack," said Logan.

"What about water balloons," said Erin.

"Or snowballs," said Zachary, "if it ever snows again."

"What if we just came up with the most shocking and amazing and completely awesome and vexylent endangered animal report ever in the history of the world instead," I said.

"That sounds good to me," said Erin.

"Okay, I guess." Zachary seemed a little disappointed.

"Let's get back to work," said Logan.

"I'll close the curtains," I said.

8

The Missing Books

We know it's time to leave for school in the morning because we hear Charlie's basketball bouncing outside our front door. Since we had his ball at our house, though, he couldn't dribble it, and we were almost late for school two days in a row. On Wednesday we race-walked the whole way, but on Thursday we had to jog.

"I'd like you to return Charlie's basketball today," said my mom.

Louie ran out of his house without his mom and Maggie, and we all started jogging again.

"I'd rather wait until he comes and asks for it back nicely," I said. "And apologizes for being in cahoots with Rosemary T."

"Dumb old Rosemary T.," said Tess.

"Teresa Louise Smith!" My mom stopped right where she was.

Uh-oh, I thought, but out loud I said, "Mom, we can't stop now." Maybe by changing the subject I could save Tess from getting in trouble.

My mom started jogging again, and we all did too. We made it to school just when the lines were heading in, so we weren't late at all. *Phew!* I do not like to go to the office and get a late slip from Mrs. Bentley, the school secretary, if I can help it. And it's not because she's mean or anything at all. It's just because I'm a very law-abiding citizen and being late is sort of against the rules.

Erin and I went to the library at first recess, but Ms. Pearl hadn't had a chance to check in all the returned books yet. She told us to come back at lunch recess, and that's just what we did as soon as we finished eating. Right when we opened the door to go in, the Rosemarys came racing out and nearly knocked us over.

"What in the world?" I said.

"Watch where you're going," said Erin.

"You watch where you're going," said Rosemary W.

"We weren't the ones running inside," I said.

They both started giggling and hurried off.

"That was close," I heard Rosemary T. say.

"That was weird," said Erin.

I just shrugged my shoulders. It seemed like almost everything the Rosemarys did was weird nowadays.

"Hi, Ms. Pearl," I said. "I'm here for the books."

"They're waiting for you right on my desk," she called from the other end of the library. "They're rubber banded together with your name on them. Why don't you look through them and decide which ones you want?"

"Okay." I glanced at her desk but didn't see anything. "Do you think it's okay if I move things?" I asked Erin.

"I'm not sure." Erin put her head close to the desk and tried to peek under some papers without touching anything.

"I don't see them, Ms. Pearl," I said.

"I'll be right there." She walked over. "They're right . . . Hmm. I thought they were right here."

She looked under some papers and then on her chair and around the floor. "That's odd."

She looked in the bin where we return books and on a rolling shelf for books that are ready to be reshelved. "Very, very odd."

"We can help," I said. "I'm sort of an expert at finding lost things."

We spread out and looked all around the library, by the computers, on all the worktables, even in the garbage cans.

"Maybe Mr. Harrison or one of the other teachers picked them up," she said. "I'll find them and bring them to your classroom. Go out and enjoy the rest of recess."

"Okay," we said, and headed outside.

When recess was over, Mr. Harrison wanted us to keep book talking. Each month we share what we're reading with the whole class. We don't have to write a report or anything; we just have to stand up and talk. And it doesn't matter if it's a book or a magazine or even the comics. I think Mr. Harrison is just checking to make sure we're reading something on our own.

So far the horsey girls' table had gone and so had the loud sports boys' table. Right now it was the smart boys' table's turn. That happens to be my table, even though I'm not a boy and am only regular-smart, not supersmart like the rest of them. I went first and told all about *The Dinosaur Mystery* and the Boxcar Children. Next went Christopher, who book talked *Tall Tales from Outer Space*, by Reed McCoy. Then Trevor told about *Fabulous Arachnids*, by L. H. Mumford. Last went Logan, who book talked *Tracking the Tyrannosaurus rex*, by Joe Thomas. I wrote down the title and author for that one because I know Tess would love me to read it to her.

Just after Logan finished, Ms. Pearl knocked on our classroom door and stuck her head in. "Sorry to interrupt. Can I have a word?" she asked Mr. Harrison.

He walked over to the door, and they put their heads together and started whispering.

"Excuse me a minute, class." Mr. Harrison stepped out into the hall with Ms. Pearl.

We all just sat there quietly. Nobody even talked or anything. Except for the Rosemarys, who were whispering together.

Finally Mr. Harrison and Ms. Pearl came back into the room.

"It seems that some important books have gone missing from the library," said Mr. Harrison. "The books were on jungle cats and were set aside for one of your classmates. Does anyone have any ideas about what might have happened to them?"

Both Mr. Harrison and Ms. Pearl stared around the classroom.

"Well," Ms. Pearl said finally. "If anyone decides they do have something to share about the missing books, please come talk to either me or Mr. Harrison."

After Ms. Pearl left, everyone was quiet for a minute. Then people started looking at each other and saying things like "I don't know what she's talking about, do you?" I knew, though. I looked at Erin, and she looked back at me.

"Rosemary T.," said Mr. Harrison.

Rosemary T. made a little gasping noise and jumped in her chair. "What?"

"Would you like to book talk next?"

After school Erin and I waited by the fence to be picked up for dance class.

"What in the world do you think happened to the books?" I asked.

"I don't know," said Erin. "Ms. Pearl and Mr. Harrison made it sound like it was something bad."

"I know. They made it seem like they were stolen or something."

"Maybe they were valuable," said Erin.

"Or maybe someone really needed them for their report," I said. "And they didn't want to wait until I'd returned them."

"Which is very dumb," said Erin. "You would have returned them on Monday, and that would have given them all week before our reports are due."

"And also," I said, "if they had asked, I would have shared."

Rosemary T.'s mom and Erin's mom both pulled up at the same time, so we had to say good-bye and get in different cars.

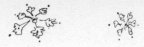

Miss Akiyama let each of us try being the Snow Princess during class. And FYI, it was a little bit of a tricky part. At the beginning you had to dance carrying a silver bucket full of pretend snowflakes. While you twirled all around, trying not to get dizzy, you had to throw the snowflakes on the tree-people to make them be able to move. Once the bucket was empty, you had to set it down, out of the way, and everyone danced together.

When class ended, everyone dashed out the door except for Hannah. She was the last person to try being the Snow Princess and was stuck picking up all the snowflakes. I felt bad for her and so I stayed behind to help.

"You were a very, extremely good Snow Princess," I said. "In fact, I think you were the best of all of us."

Hannah stopped picking up snowflakes and looked at me very surprised. "I thought you thought *you* were the best."

"I missed half the trees with my snowflakes," I said, "and they never got to join the dance."

"Rosemary T. said you did that on purpose," said Hannah.

"No way," I said. "And then I set the bucket down in the wrong place, and Rosemary W. tripped on it."

"That was on purpose, though, right?" asked Hannah.

This time *I* stopped picking up snowflakes and looked at *her* very surprised. "Why would I do that?"

"Because you want the solo part?" Hannah said, but she didn't sound so sure.

"How could I get the solo after making all those mistakes?" I asked.

Hannah stopped and thought about that a little.

"I am definitely not Snow Princess material," I said. "But you definitely are."

"Thanks," Hannah said quietly. She started picking up snowflakes again.

"Too bad this wasn't real snow," I said.

"Yeah," said Hannah. "Too bad it wasn't coming down outside, and we got to have a day off school."

"Speaking of school," I said. "Wasn't it weird when Ms. Pearl came into class?"

"Yeah," said Hannah.

"Those books she was looking for are ones I need for my report." I put the very last snowflake in the bucket. "I've been waiting for them all week, and now they're gone."

"But it doesn't really matter, right?" she asked. "Now that you're doing a different animal."

"I'm not doing a different animal," I said.

"But Rose . . . ," Hannah started.

"The next class is waiting, girls," said Miss Akiyama.

So we scurried out of the room and headed for our carpools.

9

Boy-Friends and Girl-Friends

After dinner my mom told me I HAD to bring Charlie back his basketball. And that is HAD to, with a capital *H-A-D*. And I was HORRIFIED and unHAPPY and wanted to throw a HISSY fit right then and there.

"I'll do it," said Tess.

"*Phew!* and thank you," I said.

"You can't just send Tess over," said my mom.

"Why not?" It seemed like a great idea to me. This way Charlie could get his basketball back, which was clearly important to my mom, and I wouldn't have to go to his house, which was clearly important to me.

"Because he's your friend," my mom said.

"He's not my friend!" I said. "He's a boy!"

"Can't you be friends with boys?" asked my dad.

"No!" But then I started to think about it a little bit. "I don't know. Maybe."

"What about those boys who came over the other day?" asked my mom.

"Zachary and Logan? Those are just boys I'm working on a project with."

"What about me?" asked my dad.

"You're just my dad," I said.

"Just your dad? Aren't we friends too?"

"Well, I guess we're friends too."

"So why isn't Charlie your friend?" My mom's eyebrow was going up-up-up. "You've known him your whole life."

"Well . . . " I thought very hard about all this for a minute. "I guess maybe he *used* to be my friend but not anymore. He and Rosemary T. told the whole class what my animal was. Then he spied on me! He is in cahoots with her of all the people in the world!"

"Sometimes friends mess up," said my dad.

"And the best thing to do is talk about it and figure it out," said my mom.

"Figure it out and forgive and forget," said my dad.

"I have some bad news for you," I said. "It turns out I am not at all good at talking things out with people. I tried to do that with Rosemary T. when Aunt Flora was here. I had a very serious what's what with her, but we didn't figure anything out."

"I bet you'll have better luck with Charlie," said my mom.

"I wouldn't be so sure about that," I said.

"I'm sure," said my dad.

I did a big, huge sigh. "Okay, fine." I went to get Charlie's basketball.

"Can I come?" asked Tess.

"Yes," I said.

"No," said my mom at the same time. "I think it's better if Cinderella and Charlie have some privacy."

"We do not need privacy at all," I said. "I Need Tess with me with a capital *N*."

"All right," said my mom.

"Figure, forgive, and forget!"

called my dad as Tess and I headed to the door.

I was very, extremely nervous on the walk over to Charlie's. I was not looking forward to this whole figuring-out business at all. My feet were dragging, and I could barely pick them up. Luckily Tess wasn't worried. She marched right over and rang the Princes' doorbell.

Charlie's big brother, Will, answered. "Charlie! Your girlfriend's here!" he yelled.

My cheeks got red-hot as can be. I was about to set the record straight right then and there, but Will jogged away from the door.

"I am not his girlfriend at all!" I whispered to Tess.

"You're a girl," she said. "And you're his friend. Well, you used to be."

"I don't think that's what Will meant," I said. "I think he's a teaser just like Charlie!"

And then Charlie appeared.

"Hi, Tarlie!" said Tess. "We brought back your basketball!"

"Thanks," he kind of mumbled.

I handed it to him and waited for him to say something like "Sorry for spying on you." When he didn't say anything, I started to leave, but Tess just stood there.

"Come on, Tess," I said.

"But the *f*'s," she said.

I gave her a little bit of a mean look, but then I took a big, deep breath. "Are you for some reason mad at me, Charlie? You've been acting a little weird lately."

"Like how?" he asked.

"Like spying with Rosemary T."

"It was her idea," he said.

"You didn't have to go along with it. And you and Rosemary T. ended up telling the whole class my animal. Now I can't shock and amaze anymore."

"You're still going to shock and amaze with *Zachary*," said Charlie.

"And Erin and Logan too," I said.

"Yeah, but mainly with Zachary."

"Uh-uh," I said. "We all have equal parts."

"Equal parts of what?"

I opened my mouth up to tell him, and then I remembered that he might be in cahoots with Rosemary T. "I can't tell you."

"I promise I won't tell again," he said.

I thought about that for a minute but then shook my head. "I can't. It's not just my secret this time. It wouldn't be fair to Erin and Logan and Zachary."

"And *Zachary*," Charlie said in a weird, squeaky voice.

I looked at Charlie very, extremely confused. "Okay. Well. See you later."

I turned around and started walking home, and Tess ran to catch up with me. "See?" I whispered. "I'm just not good at these things."

We got partway there when Charlie yelled, "Wait a sec!"

We stopped, and he dribbled his ball up to us. "You know dinosaurs are extinct, right?"

"Yep." This seemed like a very strange thing to say and not at all what I expected.

"And you know our report is on endangered animals, right?"

"Yep," I said again.

"Then why are you doing a report on dinosaurs?"

"Dinosaurs?" I asked.

"Yeah," said Charlie. "Rosemary T. and I saw one on your table."

"That was my Charlotte Brontosaurus," said Tess.

"Well, Rosemary T. thinks you might have switched animals so you can still shock and amaze everyone," said Charlie.

"Well, we didn't," I said.

"So you're still doing ocelots?"

I didn't say anything.

"I'm doing Komodo dragons," he said.

"Yes, I'm still doing ocelots," I said. "But don't tell Rosemary T., okay?"

"I promise," said Charlie. "I will never tell Rosemary T. another thing in my whole entire life. You can trust me from now on."

He looked very, extremely serious at me, and I looked very, extremely serious right back.

"I'm sorry I helped tell your animal," he said. "And I'm sorry I spied on you."

"I accept your apology," I said.

"Great!" He dribbled his basketball in a circle around us and then bounced it back to his house.

"Bye, Tarlie!" yelled Tess.

"See ya, Tess!" he called. "See ya, Tinder!"

I did a big, huge sigh and rolled my eyes. Maybe the next time I had a serious talk with him I'd ask him to quit calling me that name.

10

Strange and Suspicious

"Rosemary T. thinks we're doing our report on dinosaurs," I said.

"How do you know?" asked Zachary.

"Charlie told me," I said. "He is all done with being in cahoots with her."

Erin nodded. I had already told her the whole story before school. "And that is why," she all of a sudden said in a very loud whisper, "brontosaurus is no longer here today."

We stared at her all confused for a minute, but then Rosemary T. walked right by the worktable and pretended to throw something away.

As soon as she walked back past us, Erin whispered more quietly, "We might as well let her keep thinking that we're doing dinosaurs."

"Yeah," said Zachary. "Then she'll be even more shocked when she sees what we're really doing."

"I bet she's telling everyone else too," said Logan. "This is brilliant! Thanks to Rosemary T., the whole class will be amazed!"

"Let's finish up, everyone," said Mr. Harrison. "Five more minutes until lunch. And I want all your book walls put away before we go."

"Cinderella and I are going to get a stuffed toucan after school today," said Erin. "So we'll be all ready to practice tomorrow when you guys come over."

"I'll bring my gorilla," said Logan.

We went back to our desks, and I set my *Lots About Ocelots* notebook on it. Then I had a very small *aha!* I turned the notebook over so the plain back was facing up, just in case Rosemary T. happened to look.

Erin and I checked in with Ms. Pearl during lunch about the missing books. She said she hadn't found them yet and was very sorry. We told her we were very sorry too.

The end-of-recess bell rang, but I had a couple burning questions that I just had to ask. "Are they by any chance rare and valuable books?"

"Yeah," said Erin. "Would somebody want to steal them?"

"Maybe for ransom," I said, "or to sell them on the black market?"

Ms. Pearl laughed. "No, they weren't valuable like that."

"Why do you think they went missing then?" I asked.

"I hope it was just an honest mistake," said Ms. Pearl. "I hope I misplaced them or somebody picked them up by accident. I also hope they reappear in time for you to use them."

"Me too," I said. "But just in case, I'm going to the public library this weekend."

"I think that's a fine plan," said Ms. Pearl.

We were the last ones back to class, so we quick sat down. We pulled out a pencil and paper, because Mr. Harrison was starting our weekly spelling test.

Even though the spelling bee was behind us, we still had to practice every week.

"Your first word is *law*," said Mr. Harrison. "It is against the law to steal."

Erin looked over at me, and we raised our eyebrows at each other.

"Your next word is *washing*. My dad was busy washing his car."

"My dad makes me and my brother do that," said Charlie.

Mr. Harrison smiled. "*Caught.* Don't get caught cheating."

"Or stealing," said Jack.

Most teachers like a classroom to be very, extremely quiet during a test, but Mr. Harrison never seemed to mind a little bit of talking. He gave us twenty more words and finished with a bonus word: *daughter.*

"Send your papers up," said Mr. Harrison.

I passed my paper across to Christopher to take up front. Just as I did, I noticed that my *Lots About Ocelots* notebook was right side up. "That's strange."

"What is?" asked Logan.

"Did any of you turn my notebook over?" I asked my tablemates.

84

"What notebook?" asked Trevor.

"This one." I tapped my *Lots About Ocelots* notebook. "I left it upside down before lunch, and now it's right side up."

"No," said Trevor and Christopher together.

"Zat ees a leetle suspicious," Logan said in his French accent. He raised his eyebrows at me and looked over at the Rosemarys.

I did too.

I picked up the notebook to put it away in my desk, but a piece of paper sticking out of it caught my eye. I opened to that page. A note was tucked inside that said:

Don't tell anyone! I'll get in BIG trouble! Look behind E.

"What in the world?" I said very loud and surprised.

"Everything okay, Cinderella?" asked Mr. Harrison.

"No . . . I don't know . . ." Then I stopped. I didn't have any idea what the note was about, but I didn't want Erin to get in big trouble. "It's nothing."

"Okay, class," said Mr. Harrison. "How did the spelling test go for you?"

People started raising their hands and telling what words they thought were hard and what ones they thought were easy. I couldn't stop thinking about the note, though. I turned around in my seat to look behind me. The only things there were the window and the heater and a bookshelf with encyclopedias on it. Behind the window was the sky. Behind the heater was nothing, because it was stuck to the wall. I Had, Had, Had with a capital *H* to look behind the bookshelf.

I raised my hand.

"Did you have something to add, Cinderella?" asked Mr. Harrison.

"No," I said. "I think my pencil rolled under the bookshelf. Can I go look?"

"Sure." Mr. Harrison turned and started writing some spelling words on the board.

I peeked over the top of the bookshelf, but it was pushed up so close to the wall that nothing could fit behind it. I bent down on the floor to look under it.

There were a ton of dust bunnies but nothing else.

"Did you find it, Cinderella?" asked Mr. Harrison.

"I guess I don't really know what I'm looking for," I said.

"I thought you lost your pencil." He looked a little confused.

"Oh yeah. No, I didn't find it."

Rosemary W. raised her hand. "Cinderella shouldn't be out of her seat. One of her shoes is off."

I sighed and went and sat back down.

I just could not wait for school to finally end. As soon as Erin and I were alone, I practically burst out, "What in the world did that note mean?"

"What note?" she asked.

"The one you left in my *Lots About Ocelots* notebook at lunch recess."

"I didn't leave you a note," she said. "Plus, I was

with you all recess."

"Oh yeah," I said. "Well, look at this." I opened up my backpack and pulled the note out. "We have to be a little careful. Whoever wrote it is afraid they're going to get in trouble."

Erin and I bent over the note.

"'Don't tell anyone!'" she read. "'I'll get in big trouble! Look behind E.'"

I put the note back in my backpack to keep it safe, and we walked over to the fence to wait for my mom.

"That is very strange," she said.

"I know," I said. "I looked behind me in class. All there was was the window and heater and the bookshelf. And the only thing behind the bookshelf was dust."

"Who else in our class has a letter *E* name?" she asked.

We named everyone table by table, but there were no other *E*s.

"Maybe it's someone in the other third-grade class," I said, "like Emma."

"Maybe," said Erin. "We should call her and ask."

My mom pulled up in her car, and Tess waved like mad.

"This is going to drive me crazy," I said.

"Me too," said Erin.

We jumped in the car, and I climbed over Tess's car seat.

"Mall or the library first?" asked my mom.

"Mall!" we all yelled.

Luckily being at the mall with Erin and Tess and my mom somehow made me completely forget about the note, and I didn't get driven crazy at all.

11

Leopard-Print Flat

When we finally got home from shopping for a stuffed toucan and checking out jungle cat library books, my mom was too tired to even think about making dinner. We ordered a pizza and got to eat it watching Animal Planet. That was a big treat. We never, hardly ever got to eat dinner in front of the TV.

After we ate, Erin and I decided to get to work on a mural for our book report. The Group in Cahoots had decided we needed to make the classroom look jungle-y. We opened up the closet where we kept all our art supplies and got avalanched on by a whole bunch of shoe boxes.

"*Ahhh!*" we yelled.

"Everything okay?" my dad called.

"Yep!" I called back.

"What are you doing with all these shoe boxes?" asked Erin.

"I'm not sure yet," I said. "We're going to make something with them, but we don't know what yet."

We piled the boxes back up, but one of them was heavier than the rest and rattled. I opened it up, and there was my missing leopard-print flat!

"What in the world?" I said.

"It wasn't camouflaged," said Erin. "It was hiding."

I only had socks on, so I slipped the flat on my foot, and we went back to the dining-room table with construction paper and colored pens.

"Speaking of what in the worlds," I said, "I almost forgot about the note."

"Me too," said Erin.

I looked at the clock, and it was eight. "My mom will say it's too late to call Emma. We'll have to do it tomorrow."

"Hopefully she wrote it and can explain what it's all about," said Erin.

"Otherwise," I said, "it's just another mystery, like the missing books."

We started drawing the biggest trees we could on the paper. When we had a pretty good rain forest, Erin went to get her new toucan. She flew it into the dining room and pretended to land it on one of the trees.

"This doesn't look very good," she said.

"You're right," I said. "We need to make bigger trees."

"Do you have bigger paper?" she asked.

"Let's go look." Then I had an *AHA!* "Wait, I have an idea. What do you think about this?"

Logan and Zachary came over after lunch on Saturday. Tess sat at the dining-room table with us and set Charlotte Brontosaurus right in the middle. Even though the curtains were closed up tight, we couldn't be too careful.

"I had to go all the way to the downtown library yesterday, but I finally found something to check out on Pacific pocket mice." Zachary pulled two magazines out of his backpack. "I think I'm going to study these guys when I grow up. That way when another kid tries to do a report on them, he'll have an easier time."

"I might want to be a scientist when I grow up too," said Erin. "I'm not sure what I want to study, though. There's tons of stuff written about these already." She pulled the stuffed toucan we'd found at the mall out of a shopping bag.

"Here's my stuffed gorilla." Zachary plopped it in front of him on the table.

"Tess," I said. "Would you mind getting my ocelot off my bottom bunk and Tiptoe?"

"Sure!" She slid off her chair and ran out of the room.

"We went to the library yesterday too," I said. "And I got these books." I tapped a stack on the table. Underneath the books was my *Lots About Ocelots* notebook. "Oh yeah, look at this." I pulled the note out and passed it across the table.

Logan read it first. "This is mysterious."

"I know," I said. "I thought Erin wrote it, but she didn't."

"We called Emma in the other class and asked her," said Erin. "But she didn't write it either."

"And we can't think of any other *E* names," I said.

Zachary read it. "You're telling people," he said. "Even though it says not to."

"I think it's okay to tell people outside of school," I said. "You guys wouldn't get anyone in trouble, right?"

"Right," everyone said at once.

"I looked behind everything behind me in class and couldn't find a thing," I said. "And I don't even know what I'm supposed to be looking for."

"Too bad we don't know a handwriting expert," said Logan.

We all sat looking at the note for a few minutes, but that wasn't getting us anywhere.

"Let's get to work on our play," I said. "I'll worry about the note later."

Tess ran into the room and handed me my ocelot and Zachary her stuffed mouse, Tiptoe.

"Let the Group in Cahoots meeting come to order," said Logan.

"Erin and I had an idea about the tropical rain

forest," I said. "Instead of drawing a mural, what do you think about using people as trees?"

"*People?*" asked Zachary.

"Yeah," said Erin. "We know some kids in school who are experts at being trees because of dance class."

"Would they mind if Tiptoe crawled on them and maybe tried to dig under their feet?" asked Zachary.

"As long as you pick the right tree, I think it would be fine," I said. "The people we're talking about are Abby and Hannah and the Rosemarys."

"Don't try to crawl on one of the Rosemarys," said Erin. "They would freak out."

"Abby's probably the best tree for you," I said.

"But when she gets chopped down," said Zachary, "Tiptoe will have to run somewhere else."

"Hannah then," I said.

"I'm not so sure about her," said Logan. "Sometimes she's a little Rosemary-ish."

"How about Charlie?" I asked. "We could ask him to volunteer."

"And he could wear a shirt with a pocket that Tiptoe could jump into," said Erin.

"Are we sure we can trust him?" asked Logan.

"I think we can," I said.

"Who should be the guy cutting down trees?" asked Zachary.

"Maybe Mr. Harrison," I said.

We practiced all afternoon, and my mom and dad and Tess even helped. My mom and Tess were very good trees, and my dad was a vexylent woodcutter. At five o' clock all the kids got picked up, and my mom and dad and Tess and I sat down at the dining-room table to talk about dinner.

"Chinese!" said Tess.

"We ordered in last night," said my always-wanting-us-to-eat-healthy-food mom.

"Moo shu pork," said my dad.

"Fine, fine." My mom and Tess went into the kitchen to call and order.

"What's this?" My dad picked up the note that was still in the middle of the table. "'Don't tell anyone! I'll get in big trouble! Look behind E.'"

"That's . . . ," I started to say. But the way my dad read it made me hear the note differently. "Could you please read it again the way you just did?"

"'Don't tell anyone!'" read my dad. "'I'll get in big trouble! Look behind E.'"

"'Look behind E,'" I said. "Not 'Look behind, signed E.'"

My dad gave me a funny look. If he had been my mom, his eyebrow would have been way, way, way up.

"Thanks, Dad!" I jumped out of my chair. "I think I have it figured out a little bit! I have to go call Erin!"

"Let your mom order the Chinese food first," called my dad. "I'm starving!"

12

Adidas with Red Stripes

rin and I spent a ton of time on the phone that night. I read her the note the way my dad read it, and she agreed. We decided that instead of trying to figure out who wrote it, we would both make a list of everything we could think of that started with the letter *E*.

"It would make it so much easier if we knew what we were looking for," she said. "Do you think we need to look behind big things like an elephant or small things like an egg?"

"I don't know about that," I said. "But whatever we're looking for must be at school. The note was stuck in my notebook in our classroom. I'm sure I'm not supposed to go to the zoo and look behind an elephant."

"Yeah," said Erin. "I guess you're right. Should we tell Logan and Zachary and get their help?"

I thought about that a little. "Help would be good. But I really don't want to get anyone in big trouble like the note said."

"Even someone like the Rosemarys?" asked Erin.

I thought a little bit more. "Even someone like them. I think we better be supersneaky and not let anyone else know what we're up to."

On Monday morning Erin and I huddled under my umbrella before the bell rang. It was slush-puppying on us, which is like dribbly-spit, only icier.

"Show me your list," she said.

I unfolded it.

> earth − globe
>
> earthquake supplies − in the closet
>
> easel − maybe in the kindergarten classrooms?
>
> electric outlets − all over the place, but can anything fit behind them?
>
> elm trees − ask Mom if there are any around

enchilada – when will they serve them for lunch?

encyclopedias

entrance and exit – to the classroom and the school

equipment for sports – in the gym?

erasers

espresso – if Mr. Harrison drinks any

excuses for gym or being late – maybe in the office?

expelled – has anyone been expelled?

"How did you come up with so many?" asked Erin.

"I went through the dictionary," I said, "and wrote down every possible thing that started with the letter *E*."

"This is what I came up with." She showed me her list: envelopes, erasers, Elmer's glue, and earphones.

"Yours makes a lot more sense," I said.

"Yours is full of way more places to look, though," said Erin.

The bell rang, and we ran to get in line.

"Let's start looking behind things on our lists when we can," I said. "But don't look suspicious."

By lunchtime I had looked behind the globe and the earthquake supplies in the closet. I'd also

asked Mr. Harrison if he ever
drank espresso. He said he did
every morning and pointed to
the coffee cup on his desk. I
checked, and there was nothing
behind it. Erin had looked behind the
erasers and the extra Elmer's glue at the back
of the room. Neither of us had found anything
interesting. *Alas.*

After we finished eating lunch, we headed out to
the gym to look behind some sports equipment.

"I didn't want to say anything while we were
eating," said Erin, "because there were so many
people around. But I asked the lunch ladies about
enchiladas. It turns out they never serve them,
only tacos."

"I'll cross that off the list then," I said.

When we got to the gym, I tried the door, but it
was locked. Erin pulled on it hard too. Just then
Mrs. Anderson, the gym teacher, walked up.

"Do you girls need something?" she asked.

"We might have lost something in the gym," said
Erin.

"Was it one of Cinderella's shoes?" asked Mrs.
Anderson. "Like the Adidas with red stripes that

you lost last month?"

Erin looked at me, and I looked back at her.

"We're not really sure what it is," I said. "I don't think it's a shoe."

"This sounds a little fishy," said Mrs. Anderson.

"You're right," I said. "It's really more of a scavenger hunt, I guess. We're following clues."

"I see," she said. "Now it sounds kind of fun."

"It's actually a little frustrating," I said.

"Because we don't know what we're looking for," said Erin.

"Well," said Mrs. Anderson, "if I ever find anything that doesn't belong in the gym, I always put it in the Lost and Found. I haven't found anything in the past few days, though."

"Thank you," I said. "That is very, tremendously helpful."

"So glad to be of service." Mrs. Anderson unlocked the gym door and went inside.

"Vexylent," I said. "Another thing to check off the list."

"Should we go to the office next or the kindergarten rooms?" asked Erin.

But we couldn't go to either, because the bell rang.

On the way home from school I asked my mom

about elm trees. She said she knew there were several in Seattle but wasn't sure about around my school. I figured if a big plant expert like my mom didn't know where any elms were, no third grader would either. So that got crossed off the list.

Erin and I talked on the phone after dinner and decided to cross off electric outlets too. Every outlet we saw that day was screwed tight into the wall. There was no way to get anything behind one unless you shoved it into the plug openings. And that seemed a little too dangerous to look into.

At school on Tuesday we always kept our eyes open when we went through every entrance and exit. Erin pretended she needed to send a letter and asked Mr. Harrison if he had an envelope she could borrow. He did, but there wasn't anything interesting behind the pile of them. She also checked behind the earphones at the back of the room. *Alas,* nothing.

"I've finished my list," she whispered to me at

lunch. "How about you?"

"I tried to look behind the encyclopedias in the classroom," I said. "But there's no room for anything. They're pushed all the way to the back of the bookshelf."

"What do we have left?" she asked.

"We need to go to the office and ask about excuses and expelled people," I said. "We also need to go to the kindergarten classrooms."

So we headed off to see Mrs. Bentley when we finished eating.

"Hello, girls," she said when she saw us. "What can I do for you?"

"Would you mind answering a few questions?" I asked. "We're on a sort of scavenger hunt."

"I'd be happy to." She got up from her desk and came over to the counter.

"First," I said, "when kids bring in excuses for having to miss PE or school or something, where do you put them?"

"I log them in one of these notebooks." She pointed to a shelf behind her. "Then I tell the people who need to know."

I had a sneaking suspicion that she wouldn't allow us to look behind the notebooks, but I decided to

try. "Are kids ever allowed behind this counter?"

"Not unless they need to make a phone call," said Mrs. Bentley. "There's a lot of private information back here."

"Like lice," said Erin.

"Exactly." Mrs. Bentley nodded.

"Speaking of private information," I said. "You don't have to tell us any names, but could you tell us if anyone has been expelled lately?"

"This sounds more like investigative reporting than a scavenger hunt," she said.

I thought about that for a minute. "You're right. We are investigating something." I walked up closer to the counter and said very quietly, "We don't want to get anyone in trouble, so we're being very secretive."

"I see," said Mrs. Bentley very quietly back. "Then I will share that no one has been expelled all year."

"That's very good news for many reasons," I said. Erin nodded.

"Thank you for all your help." We turned to the door.

"Oh, I just thought of another *E* thing." Erin turned back. "Have we had to have an exterminator come

this year? At my old school it always seemed like we needed to get rid of something, like ants or mice."

Mrs. Bentley shuddered. "Luckily we have not."

"Thanks again," we said, and headed to the kindergarten end of the hallway.

Both of the classroom doors were locked, but then I had an *AHA!* Louie could help.

We walked outside to the kindergarten yard and stood by the fence.

"Louie!" I called. "Can you come here a minute?"

He raced over. "Hiya!"

"Hiya right back!" Then I lowered my voice. "We

have a favor, but it's a very, extremely secretive one."

Louie looked very serious at us.

"We need you to look behind the painting easels in your classroom. And we need you to ask a very trustworthy person to look behind the easels in the other classroom too."

"We don't know exactly what you're looking for," said Erin. "But if you see anything suspicious, let us know."

"Like a bomb?" asked Louie.

"No, no," I said. "It wouldn't be anything dangerous."

"I'll do it," said Louie. "I'll report back after school."

"Perfect," I said.

We walked over to our favorite bench and on the way passed the Rosemarys and Hannah and Abby playing four-square.

"Hanging out with kindergartners again, Cinderella?" asked Rosemary T.

"Every chance I get." I walked right by and didn't even stop.

"Good one," said Erin.

"It's true." I sat down on our bench. "I would much rather hang out with Louie than the Rosemarys any old day."

"Me too," said Erin. "Let's see your list."

Erin had left hers in the classroom because she'd crossed everything off. I'd started carrying mine around in my pocket, though, to check things off as I went.

✓ Earth – globe – *nothing*

✓ earthquake supplies – in the closet – *nothing*

easel – maybe in the kindergarten classrooms?

(Louie working on)

✓ electric outlets – all over the place, but can anything fit behind them? – *nothing does that we want to see.*

✓ elm trees – ask Mom if there are any around – *third graders won't recognize them*

✓ enchilada – when will they serve them for lunch? – *they don't, only tacos*

✓ encyclopedias – *no space behind*

✓ entrance and exit – to the classroom and the school – *nothing*

✓ equipment for sports – in the gym? – *nothing that doesn't belong in the gym for the past few days*

✓ erasers – *nothing*

✓ espresso – if Mr. Harrison drinks any – *he does*

every morning, but nothing's behind his cup
✓ excuses for gym or being late – maybe in the office? – *no kids allowed behind counter*
✓ expelled – has anyone been expelled? – *luckily no one has*
✓ *No exterminations either*

"We're almost finished," said Erin.

"And we haven't come up with anything," I said.

Charlie bounced his basketball over and circled the bench with it. "You guys are always over here talking in secret."

"That's because we're always in cahoots," I said.

The bell rang, and we jumped off the bench and ran with Charlie to get in line.

13

Pelican-Print Rain Boots and a Big, Huge AHA!

Wednesday morning was shivery cold. They said it might snow, so I wore warm socks inside my ladybug boots. When I met Erin on the playground, she was wearing her new pelican-print rain boots.

"I love 'em!" I said.

"Thank you, thank you."

We danced around the playground and looked for frozen puddles.

"Louie didn't find anything suspicious behind the easels," I said. "And he didn't trust anyone enough to check in the other classroom, so he did that one too."

"So we're done?" Erin stopped puddle-slipping.

"Yep," I said. "And we didn't find a thing."

"We'll never know what the note was all about." Erin looked disappointed.

"I know." I was disappointed too. "But I can't think of anything else to do. Except ask the class, but then someone would get in big trouble."

Erin looked a little hopeful.

"We don't want to do that," I said.

"I guess you're right."

"It might snow," I said to cheer her up. "And you have very awesome new boots!"

She smiled, and we danced in our boots over to our line.

"Let's start our morning with some division," said Mr. Harrison. "Please pull out your math journals and copy this problem." He started writing on the board.

I wrote: *Sara is putting away books in the library. She can fit fourteen books on each shelf. How many shelves will she need to put away ninety-seven books?*

"Show your work," said Mr. Harrison. "Then draw a picture of the solution."

Mr. Harrison was very into teaching different ways to do math, so I was ready for this.

First I wrote out the problem the regular way: *97 ÷ 14.* I did the division, and the answer was 6 and 13/14ths. Then I wrote: *Sara needs seven shelves. Six will be all full, and one will only have thirteen books on it.* Next I drew a picture of a bookcase with seven shelves. I drew fourteen books on every shelf but the top one. On that one I drew thirteen.

"How many people are still working?" asked Mr. Harrison.

Lots of people raised their hands, so I decided to make my bookshelves a little more interesting. I wrote a teeny-tiny title on the first book, *Ramona the Pest.* Then I wrote a teeny-tiny author name, B. Cleary, because I couldn't fit her whole first name. Looking at all ninety-seven books I had to fill in, I started to worry I might run out of titles. Then I remembered there were a whole bunch of Ramona books. I filled the whole top shelf full of them, all together just like in a real library.

"Are we still working?" asked Mr. Harrison.

"I need some help," said Olivia.

"Me too," said a lot of other people.

Mr. Harrison started walking around the classroom giving help, and I started working on my second shelf. I decided to make this a *D* shelf since the shelf above was all *C*s for *Cleary*. I wrote *Dr. Doolittle* and pretended that was the author's name too. Then I made up a book called *Daddy Long Legs* and another one called *Dogs Are the Best*. Then I filled the whole rest of that shelf with books about dogs.

Mr. Harrison was still busy, so I started on the next shelf, shelf *E*. I made up a book called *Excellent Elephants*, by E. Emory. Then *Exciting Eggs*, by Eggbert. Then *The Truth About Glue*, by Elmer; then *Excuses and More Excuses*, by Ellie. Then I had a big, huge *AHA!* It was so big and huge that it popped out of my mouth very, extremely loud.

"*AHA!*"

"Have you had a breakthrough, Cinderella?" asked Mr. Harrison.

"I really think I have!" I said.

The classroom phone rang, and Mr. Harrison went to answer it.

"Erin," I whispered over to her table. "I think I might have figured it out!"

I think she thought I was talking about the math problem, because at first she didn't seem very excited. Then her mouth and eyes opened big and wide.

"Class," said Mr. Harrison. "I have some bad news. The school is going to close today at noon. A snowstorm is on its way."

"Hurray!" the whole class yelled.

"You don't seem too upset," he said.

"We're not!" yelled Jack.

"We're the opposite!" yelled Zachary.

"The exact opposite!" yelled Charlie.

I myself was a little bit upset, however. I Needed to get up to the library with a capital *N* before the school sent us home. I raised my hand. "Mr. Harrison, may I go up to the library really quickly? I have something I need to check on before I go home."

"Certainly," he said.

"Can Erin come too?" I asked.

"Certainly again," said Mr. Harrison.

I stood up.

"Cinderella doesn't have her shoes on," tattled Rosemary W.

We race-walked up to the library, and on the way I explained. "I think maybe, just maybe, the *E* we're supposed to look behind might be the *E* section in the library!"

"The *E* section!" said Erin. "How did you think of that?"

"I was drawing a library shelf for the math problem, and I was drawing the *E* section where all the *E* books live, and I had an *AHA!*"

"I heard that *AHA!*" said Erin.

"And the books got lost in the library," I said.

"Wait!" Erin stopped in the middle of the hall. "The books? You think the note was about the missing library books?"

"I think maybe." We started race-walking again.

"Remember that day?" said Erin. "Remember we were on our way into the library and the Rosemarys almost knocked us over?"

"Yep," I said.

"And remember it was right then that the books were gone?"

"Yep."

"I bet you're right!" she said.

We burst through the library door. A whole class of first graders turned and looked at us. Ms. Pearl stopped reading.

"Sorry," we whispered.

Ms. Pearl nodded and started reading again.

We tiptoed over to the bookshelves and followed along looking at the authors' last names—Ahlberg, Anderson, Avi; Barden, Baskin, Birney, Blume; Cleary, Cooper, Cushman; Dahl, Day—until we got to the *E* section. Eastman, Edwards, Emberley, English, Evans, etc.

I looked at Erin, and she looked at me. She crossed her fingers and arms in front of her. Then she crossed her eyes too. I giggled a little, held my

breath, and reached behind *E*.

"What in the world?" My fingers found a bunch of books attached to each other. I eased them over the regular *E* books. I was holding five books on jungle cats, rubber banded together with a note that said: reserved for Cinderella Smith.

Erin and I gasped at the same time.

"Everything okay over there, girls?" called Ms. Pearl.

"Yes!" we called back. "We mean yes," we said quieter. We did not want to give those little kids any bad ideas.

"All right, first graders." Ms. Pearl stood up. "Time to get you back to class."

As she walked past with the line of first graders, I waved the books at her. Her mouth popped open. "Can you wait for me? I'll be right back."

I nodded.

"Those creepy Rosemarys," said Erin. "I just know they hid them from you."

"There's no way to prove it, though," I said.

"Quick, put the books down!" said Erin. "Maybe we can get fingerprints!"

I set the books down on Ms. Pearl's desk just as she walked back in.

"Where did you find them?" she asked.

"Behind the *E* section," I said.

"Where?"

"Right here." I walked over and showed her. "They were hiding behind these books."

"How did you think to look for them there?" she asked.

I thought for a minute and then decided to tell the truth. I was tired of lying about scavenger hunts and investigations. "I got a note. It said: 'Don't tell anyone! I'll get in big trouble! Look behind *E*.' Erin and I looked behind every *E* we could think of, and then I suddenly thought of the *E* section in the library."

"Can I see the note?" asked Ms. Pearl.

"It's down in my backpack," I said. "But I really don't want to get anyone in trouble. Whoever left me the note was trying to help."

"True." Ms. Pearl got very quiet. I could tell she was thinking hard about something. "Well, would you like to check these out now that we finally have them back?"

"Actually I don't need to," I said. "I was able to get some from the public library."

"Okay then," said Ms. Pearl. "I guess I'll shelve

these where they really belong before the snow
sends us home for the day."

We all looked out the window. The snow was
really coming down now.

"Thank you, girls, for finding these."

"You're welcome," we both said, and race-walked
back to class.

14

Animal-Print Ballet Flats, New Blue Ballet Flats, and High-Top Basketball Shoes

We had a no-school snow day on Thursday, but it didn't really count. There wasn't any snow on the ground to play in, only dangerous ice on the roads. Dance class ended up being cancelled too, so it turned into a pretty boring day. I talked to Erin on the phone a lot about our report and went next door to ask Charlie if he would volunteer to be a tree. He said he'd be happy to, and he also said he himself was not bored at all. Even though it was too cold outside to practice basketball, he needed the extra day to finish his report.

The next day the ice had melted off the streets, which was a very, extremely good thing. It was Endangered Animal Report day, and I could not wait. We started up right away with Olivia telling about the Eriskay pony. Then Kristy told about the Cleveland Bay horse. Katie brought in a poster on bats and bat-shaped cookies too. Yum! There were dioramas on elephants and bears, and oral reports on monkeys and penguins. Charlie did a PowerPoint on Komodo dragons; and Tom, who sits next to him, told all about bees.

I myself was very shocked and amazed to hear how many different kinds of bees there are and that lots of them are endangered. That was probably my most favorite report so far, although I did like Rosemary

T.'s outfit. She was telling us about jaguars right now and had on a skirt dotted with animal spots and a vest that looked like lion fur and tan ballet flats with more black spots all over them.

"And that is the most important reason why jaguars are endangered today." Rosemary T. did a little bow, and we all clapped.

"Are there any questions or comments for Rosemary T.?" asked Mr. Harrison.

Jack raised his hand. "What amazed you the most about them?"

"Everything," she said.

"Why did you wear jaguar clothes since they're so endangered?" asked Casey.

"I'm very shocked about that, by the way," said Zachary.

"They're not real jaguar clothes," said Rosemary T.

"But still," said Jack.

"I like what Rosemary T.'s wearing," I said before I really thought about what I was doing.

"You do?" Rosemary T. looked at me like she could not believe her ears.

I sort of wished I hadn't opened up my big mouth. I really was not a big Rosemary T. fan, especially since she had most likely hidden the books I needed.

Now that I'd started, though, I might as well finish.

"Yes, I do. It shows that you can wear animal stuff without hurting any animals. I myself have a pair of fake leopard-skin flats."

"Brilliant observation, Cinderella," said Mr. Harrison. "And brilliant choice in clothing, Rosemary T."

Rosemary T. and I smiled a little bit at each other. So far, this was the most shocking and amazing thing of the whole day. Maybe of the whole school year even.

"Okay," said Mr. Harrison. "Let's continue on. Since we lost yesterday to snow, we have a lot to fit in."

Christopher did a PowerPoint on the Indian rock python, and Trevor shared a poster on the Aruba Island rattlesnake. We were all very shocked and amazed when Casey told about snow leopards, because we were all just sure she would do an endangered horse like Olivia and Kristy. Rosemary W. did another jaguar report, and Abby and Hannah did a huge poster on the very darling red panda.

Finally it was time for us, the Group in Cahoots.

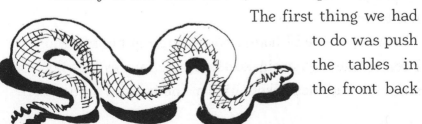

The first thing we had to do was push the tables in the front back

a ways to make more room.

Rosemary W. raised her hand. "Cinderella doesn't have her shoe on."

"Oops." I raced back to my seat and slipped on my new blue ballet flats. Then I faced our audience. "We are going to do a play for you about our endangered animals. First, though, we would like some volunteers from the audience."

Trevor raised his hand. "Do we get to be dinosaurs?"

"No," said Zachary, "you get to be trees."

"We need to make a jungle of trees for our animals to live in," said Erin.

"We would love it if any of the trees from dance class want to come up," I said.

Abby and Hannah came up front and stretched out their arms like branches.

"That's perfect," I said.

Charlie raised his hand. "I'll be one."

"Me too," said Olivia and Kristy at the same time.

"That's good," said Logan. "Now let's begin 'The Story of Limited Resources.'"

The class got quiet.

"Once upon a time there was a tropical rain forest all full of animals," I said.

Jack raised his hand. "Is this in the dinosaur age?"

"No, it's in today's time," I said. "And please hold all your questions and comments until the end."

Erin reached into the big garbage bag we brought and pulled out her stuffed toucan. "There was a toucan that lived up high in the canopy. She had a very big beak that she used to eat fruit, insects, small lizards, and eggs."

Erin flew her toucan over to Abby and sat it on

her head. Everyone laughed.

"And there was a gorilla that lived on the forest floor." Logan pulled his stuffed gorilla out of the bag and had him walk around the trees. "He weighed between three hundred and fifty and six hundred pounds, and ate about seventy pounds of food a day." He leaned the gorilla against Charlie's legs.

"And there was an ocelot." I pulled out my stuffed ocelot and jumped it from one person's arm-branch to another. "She spent most of her time in the understory of the forest and weighed about twenty-five pounds. She was a vexylent hunter and especially loved to eat rodents." My ocelot ended up on Olivia's shoulder and I cuddled it up against her neck.

"Then one day a very lost Pacific pocket mouse came to the tropical rain forest. He really belonged in California, so maybe he was on vacation or something. I don't know." Zachary pulled Tiptoe out of the bag and had him scurry all over the place. "He liked to hang out mainly in burrows in the forest floor, but he would scavenge all over the forest for things to eat. One day while he was looking for some lunch, by accident he met an ocelot."

Zachary ran Tiptoe into my ocelot on Olivia's shoulder, and I made a huge growl.

"Oh no," said Olivia.

"Oh no is right," I said. "It was lunchtime for the ocelot too, and she wanted to eat that Pacific pocket mouse."

Me, holding my ocelot, chased Zachary, holding Tiptoe, all around the classroom.

"Run, mouse, run!" yelled people in the class.

When we raced through the tree where Erin's toucan was sitting, Erin made a squawk and moved to a different tree. When we chased by Logan and his gorilla, Logan made a grunt and moved off too. Finally Zachary and Tiptoe came to the Charlie tree.

"Luckily, before he could get eaten, the Pacific pocket mouse found the perfect place to hide." Zachary popped Tiptoe into the pocket of Charlie's shirt with his head sticking out, and everyone laughed and clapped.

"*Phew!*" said Zachary.

"Rats!" I said.

"You mean 'mouse,'" said Mr. Harrison.

Everyone laughed the loudest at that.

"Now you probably think that's the end of the story, and the mouse was safe and sound," said Erin.

"But it's not," said Logan. "A person who lives

in the tropical rain forest had a family he needed to take care of. One of the ways he could earn money was by chopping down trees."

"You're on, Mr. Harrison," said Zachary.

Mr. Harrison got up from where he was sitting and walked up to the front of the room, pretending to swing an ax.

"He took his ax and got to work," I said. "He chopped down an Abby tree and a Hannah tree."

Mr. Harrison pretended to chop down Hannah and Abby, and I whispered to them to fall. When Hannah fell, Erin and her toucan, who was sitting on Hannah's head, squawked again and flew off to Charlie's head.

"Then he chopped down an Olivia tree and a Kristy tree," said Logan.

Logan's gorilla lumbered over and sat by Charlie's feet again. I jumped my ocelot to Charlie's shoulder and pretended to stare at his pocket. Erin squawked and looked down at my ocelot from her head perch.

"Man," said Charlie. "Am I a popular tree or what?"

Then Mr. Harrison came up to him with his pretend ax.

"Don't do it!" yelled Jack from the audience.

"But I need to feed my family," said Mr. Harrison.

"Figure out another way!" yelled Casey.

"What else can I do?" asked Mr. Harrison.

"Get a paper route!" yelled Trevor.

"Walk dogs!" yelled Abby from where she was lying on the floor.

"I saw a help wanted sign at Ace Hardware!" yelled Tom.

"Be an Avon Lady!" yelled Rosemary T. "I mean an Avon Man!"

"I'm not sure any of those jobs are available in a

tropical rain forest," said Mr. Harrison.

"Well, find something that is!" yelled Christopher.

"Yeah," said Olivia, "like maybe taking care of the animals there or something."

"I think you need to assign us another research report," said Christopher, "on how to save the rain forest."

"Yes! Yes!" yelled most of the class.

Mr. Harrison looked very surprised. "I think the Group in Cahoots might win the most-shocking-and-amazing-endangered-species report of all time. I don't think I've ever heard a class so enthusiastic about doing a second report before!" He bounced up and down on his toes and smiled like you wouldn't believe.

And that seemed to me to be the perfect place to end our play. We got all the chopped-down trees to stand up and hold hands. Even Mr. Harrison joined our line.

"That is 'The Story of Limited Resources,'" said Logan.

"The end," we all said together, and bowed to our audience.

The class clapped and cheered.

"We have just a few more minutes until school's

over," said Mr. Harrison. "Let's get this place cleaned up."

Everyone pitched in and helped move the tables and chairs back where they belonged. Somehow, though, with all the confusion, one of my new blue ballet flats went missing. *Alas.*

Mr. Harrison usually didn't get too worked up about stuff like this, but today he did. "Cinderella, I will not let you walk home with just one shoe on a day like this."

I looked out the window. It was sort of slush-puppying outside.

"Can you call home and get your mom to pick you up by car?" he asked.

"I bet she's already on her way," I said.

"Well, maybe we can rig you up something with a plastic bag and some tape." Mr. Harrison started looking around his desk.

"I know," said Charlie. "I can give her a piggyback ride. I live right next door to her."

"No way!" I said.

"And I have gloves," said Zachary. "You could wear one on your foot so it didn't get cold while Charlie carries you."

"No, no way!" I said again.

"Maybe my mom can drive her," said Rosemary T.

What in the world? I looked at Rosemary T. all full of surprise. Maybe she felt bad about hiding the books and was trying to make up for it. Or maybe she was being nice because I said I liked what she was wearing.

The surprise on Rosemary W.'s face was even bigger. "You're coming over to *my* house after school to spend the night. *Remember?*"

"That's right," said Rosemary T.

"We can give you a ride," said Erin. "Oh wait, no we can't. I'm coming over to your house."

"I know!" Charlie plowed through his duffel bag. "I have the best idea yet!" He pulled out a pair of high-top basketball shoes. "You can wear one of these. I brought them for basketball practice one day and forgot them."

It did seem like the best idea so far. I sat down, and he slipped one of his shoes on me. Then he tied up all the laces just like when you go to the shoe store. I stood up. The shoe was a little big, but because of all the laces it stayed on just fine and dandy.

"Thanks, Charlie," I said.

"Yes, thanks," said Mr. Harrison. "Now that the disaster has been averted, let's line up."

My mom and Tess and Mrs. Thomas and Maggie and Louie were waiting outside in the cold and wet. They looked a little miserable, so Erin and I quick jogged over. By the time we got to them, my mom's eyebrow was way, way up.

"What in the world?" She stared down at my feet.

Everyone looked, too, and Charlie bounced his basketball over to us.

"Is that yours, Tarlie?" asked Tess.

"Yep," he said.

"Why is Cinderella wearing it?" asked Louie.

"I'll give you one guess." Charlie dribbled his basketball all around us. "And I'm not letting it out of my sight. I don't want her to lose one of my shoes too."

"Cinderella." My mom's eyebrow stayed way up.

"They were brand-new."

I felt very, extremely bad and looked down at my mix-matched feet.

"Don't worry, Mrs. Smith," said Charlie. "I'll help Cinderella find it on Monday."

I looked up.

"It's in the classroom somewhere," said Erin. "It will be easy. I'll help too."

My mom's eyebrow went down. "All right." She started walking home with Mrs. Thomas, and Maggie and Louie and Tess followed.

I smiled at Erin and Charlie. "Thanks, guys." I gave them a thumbs-up, and they gave me one back. Then we raced to catch up with the others and thumbs-up-bumped the whole way home.

Read about Blackberry Lane's spunky and lovable third-grader,

Cinderella Smith

HARPER
An Imprint of HarperCollinsPublishers

www.harpercollinschildrens.com

Simon Fairfield Public Library
PO Box 607
Douglas, MA 5|0\|13
01516